T0142631

Little James' Big Adventures

Ireland
Janine Iannelli

Illustrated by: Michelle Iannelli

To order additional copies of this book, contact:
Xlibris
844-714-8691
www.Xlibris.com
Orders@Xlibris.com

ISBN:	Softcover	978-1-6698-2014-7
	Hardcover	978-1-6698-2015-4
	EBook	978-1-6698-2013-0

Print information available on the last page

Rev. date: 04/20/2022

This book is dedicated to Gabriella Gerbino.

Gabbi, you started as my teacher, became my confidant and role model, and now you are a lifelong friend. You taught me so much, and you are part of the reason why I have this love for culture, travel, and language.

Thank you!

Little James dreams of places far far away,

That he hopes to visit and see one day.

Most people take planes or even a boat,

But this little boy travels differently than most.

2

It's kind of a secret so sshh don't tell,
But Santa Clause made it with a magic Christmas spell!

The adventure starts early as James slips out of bed,
He wakes his sister gently with a small kiss on her head.

Susie wakes up smiling, "Are we going somewhere today?"
James pulls out the globe and Susie yells, "Hurray!"

"Quiet," says James, "don't make any noise,"
"The globe only works in secret, it's not like other toys!"

They place their hands on the globe
and gaze at the world inside,
"To Ireland!" James shouts, "is where we wish to ride!"
The walls start to tremble, then the floor opens wide,
James and Susie hold hands to get ready for the ride.

"Wheeee!"

The first official language of Ireland is Irish, (also known as Gaelic) although English is spoken most often.

The city of Dublin comes from the Gaelic words, 'Dubh Linn' which means, black pool.

Then suddenly it's still, they feel ground beneath their feet,
When they open up their eyes, oh what a treat!

"We're in Dublin!" James shouts, "That's Dublin castle ahead!
And the grass is so green here just like I read."

On the orders of King John of England, Dublin castle was built in 1204 on land that had previously been settled by the Vikings.

They stare up at the castle, it is old and historic,
How lucky they are to stand right before it.

The castle is sprawling and so very big,
They have to walk about to see the whole thing!

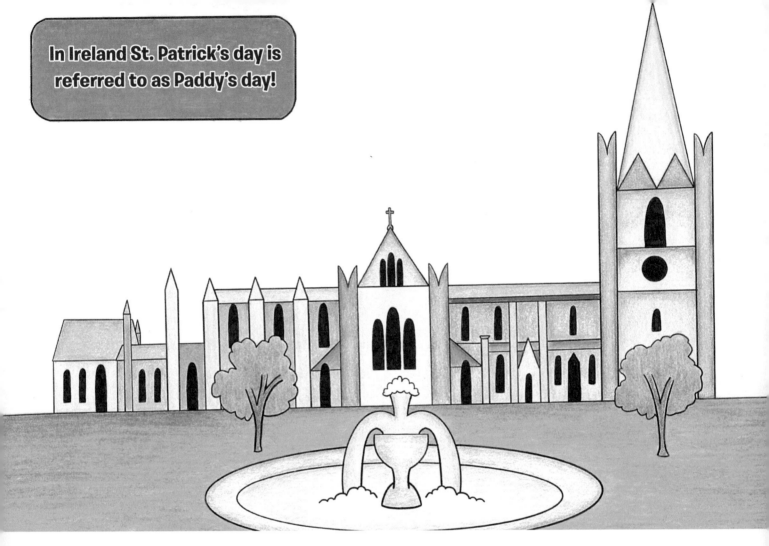

"We're off to a great start," James says with glee.
"And while we are here, St. Patrick's we should see!"

They arrive at the cathedral, what an impressive sight,
Susie stares up in awe, "It looks like a castle too, right?"

James laughs and nods his head, "I guess it does a bit.
Let's go on inside though, you know this isn't it."

10

Ireland is called the Emerald Isle because it is very green due to lots and lots of rain. Ireland typically gets around 270 days of rain a year!

"Woah," they both gasp as they walk on in.
"It's so detailed!" They say looking up with a grin.

"Next let's go to Galway," James says with a smile,
"I really like exploring this beautiful emerald isle!"

They land in the streets of Galway, Susie says, "What a lively city!
And the cobblestone roads and storefronts
make it look so very pretty."

"I like this town too, I think it's really neat!
I also think it is time we get something to eat."

"Oh yes!!" Susie smiles, "And I know what we should try!
Chipper!" She says, "It's potatoes and fish they fry."

They walk with their food and Susie rubs her tummy,
"I'm glad I got it with salt and vinegar, it makes it extra yummy."

"Now let's visit a gaeltacht while we are here.
I believe there's one not far from here."

"What's that?" Susie asks, "I've never heard this before."
"It's a place where Irish is spoken much more."

13

They place their hands on the globe, and in seconds flat,
They arrive in Connemara, it's as easy as that!

They land in a town center, it's a lovely sight,
The storefronts are unique, colorful, and bright.

They both start to walk and look all around,
James asks Susie, "Hey, what's that sound?"

They hear people laughing and the sound of rhythmic stomping,
They hear clanking, and cheering, and no sign of it stopping.

They walk around the corner and what do they see?
Heaps of people step dancing, it's an Irish céilí (kay-lee).

A céilí is a gathering where people have fun and dance,
"It does look fun James!" Susie's feet start to prance.

Ireland has many slang phrases, the most popular being the term, "Craic" which means, fun, good times, or gossip. "What's the craic?" = "What's the gossip/news?"

Susie's feet are tip tapping, tip tapping away,
A girl sees her dancing and shouts out, "Fair play!"

"That means very good!" James tells Susie,
She's so flattered her cheeks turn bright ruby.

Cara in Irish means friend.

"I'm Cara," says the girl as she comes to say hello,
"I can tell you're not from here, anything you want to know?"

"Thank you," they say, "well what should we see?"
"There's a beach nearby, you can both follow me!"

"Dia duit," Cara says to people passing by,
"Here in the Irish gaeltacht that's how we say hi."

"You speak Irish?" James asks, "That's why we wanted to visit!"
"Cupla Focal," she says, "which means, just a little bit!"

They arrive at the beach and admire what they see
The water is blue-green and clear as can be!

It's tropical even to both their surprise,
"Thank you" they say, "It's a treat for the eyes!"

"We're so glad we met you but we must say goodbye,"
"We have many more things to do here and try."

The Cliffs of Moher are approximately 14 km long (0.6 miles), and are 214 meters (just above 700ft) at their highest point.

The Cliffs are made of sandstone and shale. It is estimated that they were formed over 320 million years ago.

They take one last look, then on the globe they place their hands,
"The Cliffs of Moher!" James says, and guess where they land!

Pa poompf! Into a boat the two of them fall,
Then the boat whizzes past the tall cliff wall!

"Oh wow, there it is! And gosh what a view!"
James and Susie stare in silence, there's nothing more to do.

For nearly 20 years there was a dolphin in the dingle peninsula in Ireland that the locals named Fungie. He loved people and would always say hello to boaters. He was beloved by locals and tourists alike.

"Oh my James look, look down and see!
There are dolphins swimming right next to you and me!"

"What, are you kidding? That I did not expect!"
"But we must get going, Blarney Castle is next!"

James pulls out the globe and takes Susie's hand,
And in the blink of an eye the two of them land.

They look up at Blarney Castle, set to kiss the Blarney Stone,
"We must climb to the top, but at least we're not alone."

They both hold hands and run up to the castle,
They start climbing the stairs, it's a bit of a hassle!

The stairs are all stone, its narrow and winding,
They take a few breaks and then keep on grinding.

22

They get to the top, they are finally there!
They enjoy the quiet for a moment and the wind in their hair.

It's misty and foggy, but the green is so bright,
It's cool and calming, a beautiful sight.

Kissing the Blarney stone is said to give a person, "The Gift of Eloquence," or simply put, "The Gift of Gab."

"Now time to kiss the Blarney Stone, come on let's go!"
But when Susie sees how it is done she tells her brother, "No!"

"I'm not going upside down and from all the way up here!"
James consoles his sister, "Aw, I forgot it's heights you fear!"

"But don't worry, there is a man up here to spot us.
He'll hold your hand and so will I, you just have to trust us."

Susie is reluctant but at last she says, "Let's do it!"
They kiss the stone together, James
says, "I knew you could do it!"

Yer man turns and says, "Now go get some 99's!"
Susie turns to James, "That means it's ice cream time!"

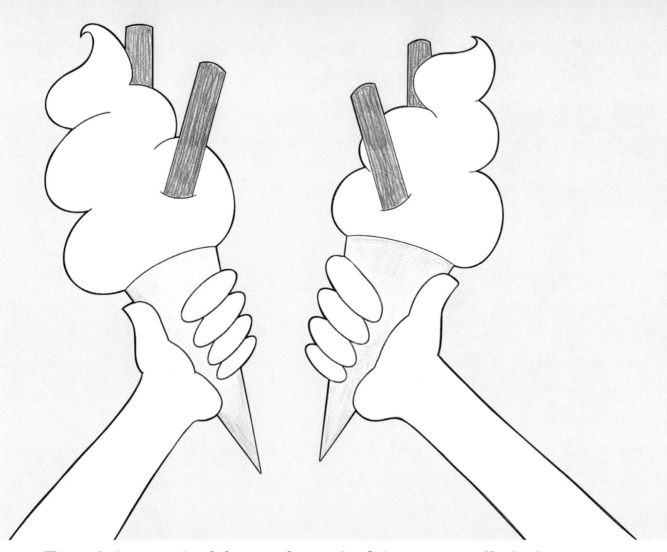

The globe works it's magic and with one small shake,
They are eating ice cream cones with yummy Cadbury flake.

This ice cream's soft and creamy and the flake is a treat,
It's so rich and delicious, dairy here just can't be beat.

Now before we head home there is one more place to see,
"Hill of Tara" James shouts, "is where we want to be!"

The Hill of Tara is Ireland's oldest ringfort! There are many all throughout Ireland. They are considered sacred and believed to be a place to spot fairies.

They fall through the air, then time slows down,
They admire from the air, the round green mounds!

They land in front of a tree, a tree filled with things!
It's filled up with gifts that everyone brings!

"This is the fairy tree Susie, we must make a wish!
We must make a wish and then leave a gift!"

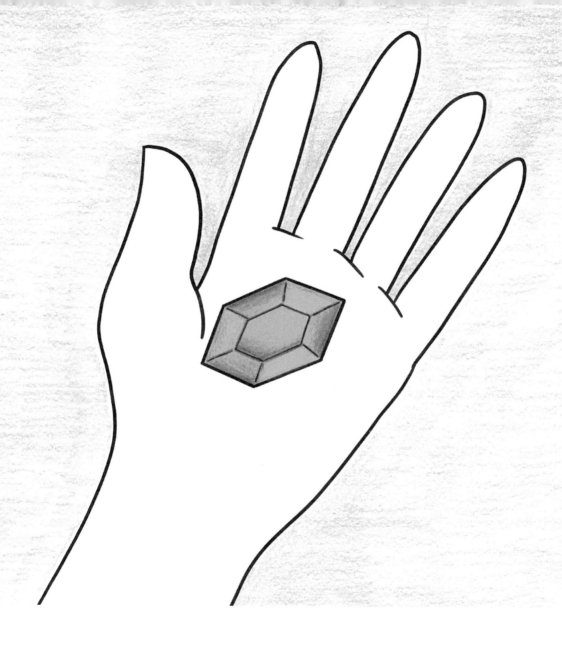

Susie goes in her pocket and pulls out a gem,
"It's my lucky rock," she explains, "it'll be a good gift for them."

They make their wishes and then it's time to head back!
They say, "Home sweet home," and they hear the ground crack!

They're whirling and twirling all through the air,
They both laugh and smile as the wind blows their hair!

Then plop! They each land in their cozy little room,
"Uh oh," James says! "It will be our bedtime soon!"

"What? Are you kidding, that is great news!"
Susie hops right in bed, "I could use a good snooze."

Map of Ireland

The Republic of Ireland and Northern Ireland were once all considered Ireland until they separated in 1922. Northern Ireland decided to stay part of the United Kingdom whereas the rest of Ireland separated from the United Kingdom and became the Republic of Ireland.

Find out where Little James' magic
snow globe takes him next!
LittleJamesBooks.com

Printed in the United States
by Baker & Taylor Publisher Services